Splish Splash

Splish Splash

poems by
Joan Bransfield Graham

illustrated by
Steve Scott

SCHOLASTIC INC.

New York Toronto London Auckland Sydney
Mexico City New Delhi Hong Kong

ISBN 0-439-13349-1

Text copyright © 1994 by Joan Bransfield Graham. Illustrations copyright © 1994 by Steve Scott. All rights reserved. Published by Scholastic Inc., 555 Broadway, New York, NY 10012, by arrangement with Ticknor & Fields Books for Young Readers, A Houghton Mifflin company.

SCHOLASTIC and associated logos are trademarks and/or registered trademarks of Scholastic Inc.

12 11 10 9 8 7 6 5 4 3 2 1   9/9 0 1 2 3 4/0

Printed in the U.S.A.   14

First Scholastic printing, September 1996

With love and thanks always
to my parents,
Dorothy and Carroll Bransfield,
who gave me an ocean,
and to Jim,
Heather, and Aimee,
adventurous sailors all

J.B.G.

With love to my parents,
Jean and Bill Scott,
who gave me the encouragement,
and to David Saylor,
who gave me the opportunity

S.S.

WATER

Water is a magic potion,
 it can fill a glass, an ocean,
raging river, tiny tear,
 drops of dew that disappear.
Water often spells surprises
 with its changing forms and sizes,
rain and snow, ponds and brooks,
 water has so many looks,
sounds and moods and colors—yet
 in every shape, it's always WET!

CLOUDS

Up in the air, a gathering
of water drops, a crowd,
a huddling, a puddling,
just dampness is allowed

from lakes and ponds, many places—
too many to keep track—
but when it rains and rains and pours,
clouds

put the water back!

OCEAN

A wave sneaks up to snatch my toes
then turns around and back it goes.
Next a splash to wet my legs . . .
"Come out, come out," each breaker begs.
Push and pull, "Okay, you win!" Skip, flop,

PLOP!.   Now I'm ALL in!

CROCODILE TEARS

Oh, crocodile poor crocodillo
cried so hard you soaked your pillow

kept it up for such a while

that's how we got the r i v e r i z e

WATERFALL

a water-
fall
is very
tall
it starts
out
at the
top
it falls
and
falls and
falls
and falls
until
it has to
STOP
and then it
does

a kind of HOP a CRASH a SMASH

a giant SPLASH!

!SPRINKLER!

Don't simmer
in the summer
slip into the shade
shimmy
through the sprinkler
sipping lemonade
wiggler
under wavy water
giggle in the sun
summer is
a special time
for shady wadey fun!

COOLCOOLCOOLCOOLCOOL!

ICE CUBES

ice cubes
clicking
clatter
clink

crazily
inside
my drink

crystal
chorus
clear
and bold

chattering
about
the cold

POPSICLE

popsicle
popsicle
tickle
tongue fun
licksicle
sticksicle
please
don't run
dripsicle
slipsicle
melt, melt
tricky
stopsicle
plopsicle
hand all
sticky

RAIN

rain
has washed
the world today
the green's
a greener
GREEN

the
under- and
the outerwear
and all that's in
between is in-
side out-
side

CLEAN!

BABBLING BROOK

babble
banter
burble
blab
prattle
tattle
gossip
gab
mutter
murmur
mumble
hey
please
speak up
what
did
you
say?

POOL

A pool is full of
cool green shimmer
an invitation for
a swimmer,
it just sits there
plain and flat until
I jump or dive in—
SPLAT! Then I can
feel slippery free,
be anything
I want to be—a seal,
a fish, a bobbing boat,
or just roll on my
back and float.

HAIL

a
rain
of
ice
such
tiny
balls

that
ping
and
pong
upon
the
w a l l s

that
bounce
around
out
on
the
l a w n

but
look
again
and
they're
all
g o n e

DEW

drops
of
dew

born
of
night

spark
the
day

catch
the
light

RIVER

River amble
ramble rush
more than ripples
now you push
rumble tumble
rolling roar
building into

more and more
I watch you
from a nearby shore
winding finding
forward flow
churning turning
twisting so
I want to follow
where you go . . .

STEAM

s
t
e
a
m

s
t
e
a
m

s
t
e
a
m

boil, boiling, bubbling pot
looks like it's sweaty hot
once was water, now is not
cooking is a clever shaper
turned it into water vapor

LAKE

What does it take to make a lake?
Lapping, slipping, slapping words
boating words, floating words
swishing, fishing, squishing words
wings and feathers up above, fins below,
and when the sun sinks down, a glow,
and all that rims the lake, a crown,
you see reflected upside down
in a kind of mirror glass
that ripples when the breezes pass
so many words it can take,
to start to tell about a lake

SNOW

how can
stringing
holes
together

snow
is made
of
crystal
laces

full
of frost
and
empty
spaces

SNOWSNOWSNOW
SNOWSNOWSNOWSNOW
SNOWSNOWSNOWSNOWSNOW
SNOWSNOWSNOWSNOWSNOWSN
SNOWSNOWSNOWSNOWSNOWSN

*pile up
into
so much
weather?*

*O W S N O W
O W S N O W*

POND

In summertime a pond is great for jumping into, splashing, swimming.

In wintertime
a pond's just right
    for *skating over,*
gliding, skimming.

            Soft with ripples,
                hard with ice—
            all year long
        a pond is nice.

SHOWER

a shower is
a private cloud
it is a special cloud
where I can make it
rain so hard
in such a little space

SHOWER SHOWER SHOWER

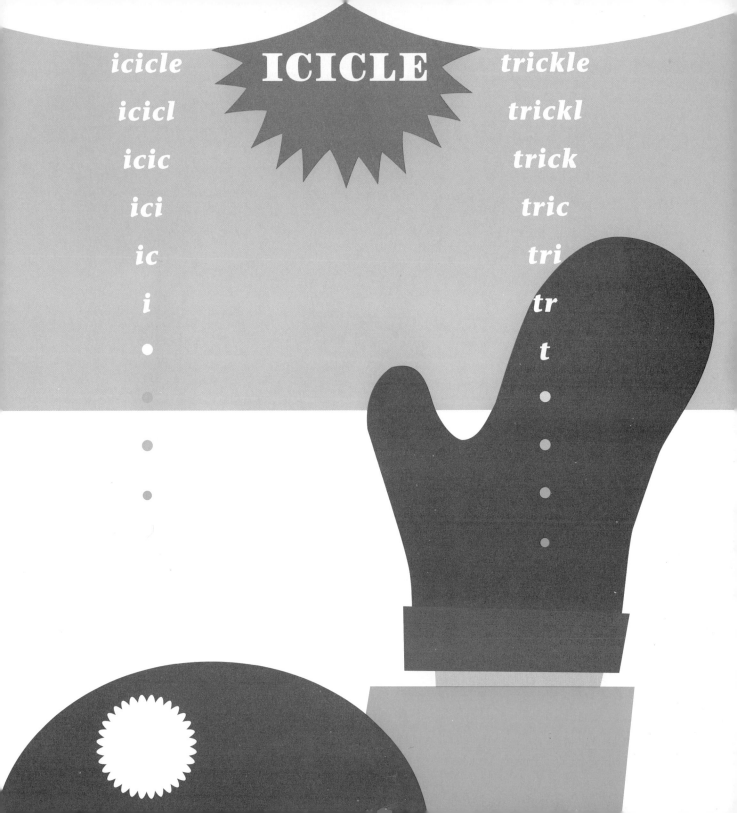

icicle **ICICLE** trickle

icicl   trickl

icic   trick

ici   tric

ic   tri

i   tr

   t

WAVE

Waves gather water building high until they break and wave good-bye